Mark Oliver

# ROBOT DOG

LITTLE TIGER PRESS
London

## LEVEL 1 For first readers

* short, straightforward sentences
* basic, fun vocabulary
* simple, easy-to-follow stories of up to 100 words
* large print and easy-to-read design

## LEVEL 2 For developing readers

* longer sentences
* simple vocabulary, introducing new words
* longer stories of up to 200 words
* bold design, to capture readers' interest

## LEVEL 3 For more confident readers

* longer sentences with varied structure
* wider vocabulary
* high-interest stories of up to 300 words
* smaller print for experienced readers

## LEVEL 4 For able readers

* longer sentences with complex structure
* rich, exciting vocabulary
* complex stories of up to 400 words
* emphasis on text more than illustrations

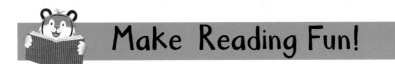 

Once you have read the story, you will find some amazing activities at the back of the book! There are Excellent Exercises for you to complete, plus a super Picture Dictionary.

But first it is time for the story . . .

# Ready?

# Steady?

# Let's read!

In a factory, on a hill,
a huge machine made
robot dogs.

The robot dogs were delivered
to new owners, who played
with them and loved them.

"I wonder what my owner will be like," said one little robot dog, as he bounced up and down on the conveyor belt.

But then, CRASH! he bounced too high and clonked his ear. Suddenly, alarm bells rang and the huge machine ground to a stop.

The machine inspected the robot dog carefully. A voice boomed:

"NOT RUSTY OR DUSTY,
NOT BATTERED OR BENT,
NO PATCHES OR SCRATCHES,
BUT THERE IS A DENT!

SCRAP!"

"So that's my name!" thought Scrap, as the machine picked him up and dropped him through a hatch.

Scrap landed in a yard
full of junk. There, staring at
him, were some other dogs.

"Hello!" he said. "I'm Scrap!
Where's my owner?

One of the dogs said, "You
don't have an owner – you're a
reject like us."

Bumper, Dent, Scratch and Sniffer
all lived in the yard. It was a
wonderful place to play.

Sometimes they played with other
dogs, who had owners. But,
after a while, they would hear,
"Dinner time!" and the dogs
would run home.

Seeing the other dogs
with their owners
made the yard dogs
feel a bit sad.

"Why don't *we* get an owner?" said
Scrap one day.

"They take a lot of looking after,"
said Bumper.

"Anyway, we can't," said Sniffer.
"We're rejects!"

"There must be a
way," thought Scrap.

"I've got an idea!"
he cried. "Come
and help!"

19

The dogs raced around collecting
anything that might be useful.

They worked all day and all night and, by the next morning . . .

. . . there stood an owner!

He was rusty and dusty,
battered and bent, patched,
scratched and covered in dents
– but he had a heart of gold.

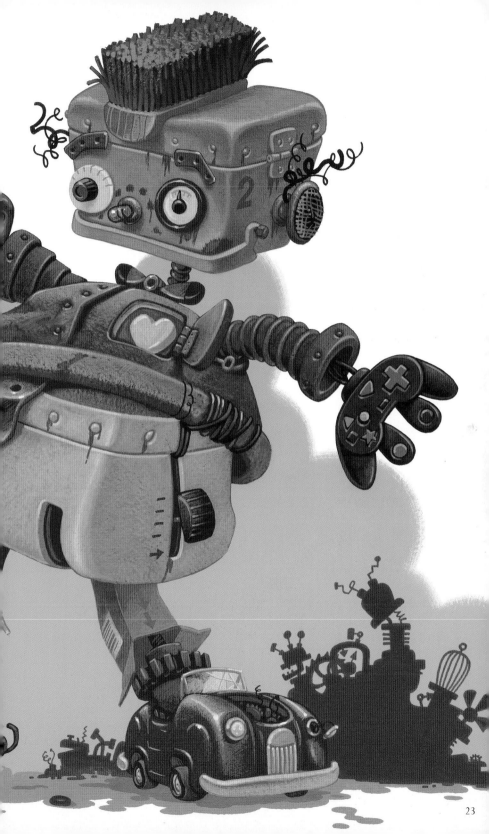

Their owner played with
them and loved them.
And the dogs were
happy at last.

25

## Excellent Exercises

Have you read the story? Well done!
Now it is time for more fun!

Here are some questions about the story. Ask an adult to listen to your answers, and help if you get stuck.

### Fun Friends

In this story, Scrap makes some really good friends in the yard. Who are *your* best friends?

### Bits and Bobs

Can you name some of the objects that the dogs used to make their owner? What would *you* use to make a robot?

## Good Dogs

Now describe what Scrap and Bumper are doing in this picture.

## Perfect Pets

Can you remember what the owner did with his dogs at the end of the story? What do *you* like doing with your pet, or a pet you know?

Can you read all of these words from the story?

**conveyor**

**factory**

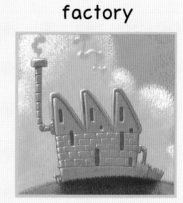

**happy**

**heart**

**home**

## idea

## inspected

## junk

## robot

## sad

Can you think of any other words that describe these
pictures – for example, what colours can you see? Why
not try to spell some of these words? Ask an adult to help!

## The Biggest Baddest Wolf

Harum Scarum is the biggest, baddest, hairiest, scariest wolf in the city. And he loves to frighten people! But when he loses his teddy, he doesn't seem so scary after all . . .

## Meggie Moon

Digger and Tiger spend all their time in the Yard. It's full of junk and it's their place. Then one day someone arrives, wanting to play . . .

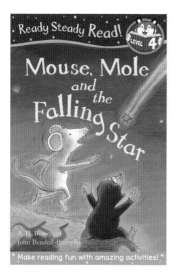

## Mouse, Mole and the Falling Star

Mouse and Mole are the best of friends. They share everything. But when a shooting star zips across the sky, they both want it for themselves. Could this be the end of a beautiful friendship?

## The Nutty Nut Chase

The animals are having a race! And the winner gets to eat a delicious, brown nut. But the race does not go as planned. And the nut seems to have a life of its own!

*To my very own 'Scrap', Lorcan – M O*

LITTLE TIGER PRESS, 1 The Coda Centre, 189 Munster Road, London SW6 6AW
First published in Great Britain 2005
This edition published 2013
Text and Illustrations copyright © Mark Oliver 2005, 2013
All rights reserved
Printed in China
978-1-84895-682-7
LTP/1800/0602/0413
2 4 6 8 10 9 7 5 3 1

# Books in the Series

## LEVEL 1 - For first readers

Can't You Sleep, Dotty?

Fred

My Turn!

Rosie's Special Surprise

What Bear Likes Best!

## LEVEL 2 - For developing readers

Hopping Mad!

Newton

Ouch!

Where There's a Bear, There's Trouble!

The Wish Cat

## LEVEL 3 - For more confident readers

Lazy Ozzie

Little Mouse and the Big Red Apple

Nobody Laughs at a Lion!

Ridiculous!

Who's Been Eating My Porridge?

## LEVEL 4 - For able readers

The Biggest Baddest Wolf

Meggie Moon

Mouse, Mole and the Falling Star

The Nutty Nut Chase

Robot Dog